By Aubrey Davis · Illustrated by Dušan Petricic

Bagels from Benny

Kids Can Press

The sun was just waking up when Benny ran
downstairs to Grandpa's bakery. He always helped
Grandpa before he went to school.

He swept the floor and dusted the shelves.
He put cookies and cakes on the counter.
He put bagels and buns in the bins.
Benny loved to help his grandpa.

People bustled in and out of Grandpa's bakery all day long. Some bought bread and some bought cake. Some bought apple strudel. Everyone bought bagels. Grandpa baked the best bagels in town.

"So crusty outside," Mrs. Silver declared.

"So soft inside," added Mr. Gold.

"You put love in your bagels," gushed Mrs. Green. "Thank you so much."

Grandpa handed Mrs. Green a bagful of bagels. "Why thank me?" he asked.

"And who else should I thank?" laughed Mrs. Green.

Just then the clock struck eight.

"We'll be late for work!" cried Mrs. Silver.

"Dear me!" gasped Mr. Gold.

"Too da loo!" sang Mrs. Green.

And they scurried out the door.

Benny was puzzled.

"Why shouldn't Mrs. Green thank you?
You make the bagels."

Grandpa lifted Benny onto the counter.

"Benny," he asked. "Aren't bagels made with flour?"

"Yes," said Benny.

"Doesn't flour come from wheat?"

"Yes." Benny nodded.

"Where does wheat come from?"

"From the earth," answered Benny.

"And who made the earth?"

"God did," Benny replied.

Grandpa smiled. "Then thank God for the bagels."

It was a good idea. Benny closed his eyes. "Thank you God," he whispered. Then he waited.

"Did He hear me, Grandpa?"

"You ask difficult questions," Grandpa chuckled. "God always hears you."

But Benny wasn't so sure. If God had really heard him, why didn't He answer?

At school that day, Benny did no work.
He didn't read and he didn't write.
At recess, he sat alone in the
shade of a tall maple tree.

"What's wrong?" asked his teacher.

"What's wrong?" asked his friends.

"I'm thinking," Benny sighed.

Benny was still thinking when
he went to bed that night.

"Maybe God didn't answer because I didn't
thank Him properly." He yawned. "Maybe
there's some other way to
thank God for His bagels."

Benny fell asleep.

Early Friday morning, a little sunbeam danced
into Benny's bedroom.

It jumped onto his pillow and tickled
his eyelids until they opened. Benny's
eyes sparkled in the sunlight.
Suddenly he had an idea.

He leaped out of bed
and ran downstairs.

That morning, Benny worked very hard in the bakery.

"Grandpa?" he asked. "Would you pay me for my work?"

Grandpa raised his eyebrows.

"Pay you? How much?"

"A big bag of bagels," replied Benny.

"Why bagels?" Grandpa asked.

"It's a secret," whispered Benny.

Grandpa laughed and gave
Benny a huge bagful of bagels.

Benny took them to the synagogue. "This is where people speak to God," he thought. "Maybe I can thank Him here."

He opened the door and peeked inside. It was dark and very still.

Benny trembled. "Maybe I shouldn't. It's not prayer time."

But Benny took a deep breath and walked in. He tiptoed past empty wooden benches. He climbed the stairs to a big wooden cupboard— the Holy Ark. His heart pounded. He could barely breathe.

"Maybe I shouldn't open it. Maybe God won't like it. The Torah is inside and it's His Special Book."

But Benny took a deep breath and pulled the doors open.

"King of the Universe," he whispered. "I brought You some bagels. I know You make them. But You never taste them, because Grandpa sells every last one."

Benny put the bag in the Ark and closed the doors.

"Thank You for making the best bagels in town," Benny whispered.

Then he ran off to school.

On Saturday, Benny and Grandpa went
to the synagogue. Everyone prayed and
sang, but not Benny. He kept his eyes
on the doors of the Ark. "Had God
eaten the bagels?" he wondered.

When the Ark was opened and the
Torah was taken out, Benny looked
inside. The bagels were gone!

His heart skipped and his eyes danced.

"I'm so glad You liked them," he
whispered. "I'll bring You more."

Week after week, Benny worked in Grandpa's bakery. Every Friday, Grandpa gave him bagels. And every Friday, Benny gave the bagels to God.

Grandpa became curious. What was his grandson doing with all those bagels?

One Friday, he followed Benny to the synagogue. He waited in the shadows and watched.

"They're still warm, just the way You like them," murmured Benny. He opened the Ark and put the bag of bagels inside.

"What are you doing?" Grandpa bellowed.

Benny spun around.

"Grandpa!" he gasped. "I'm thanking God."

"You're putting bagels in God's Holy Ark!" cried Grandpa.

"But He likes the bagels," insisted Benny.
"Every week He eats them all."

"Oh, Benny!" Grandpa laughed. "God doesn't need to eat. He
doesn't have a mouth or a stomach. He doesn't even have a body."

"He doesn't?" Benny frowned. "Then where do the bagels go?"

Grandpa looked at the Ark. He looked at Benny.
He stroked his beard and scratched his head.

"I don't know," he sighed.

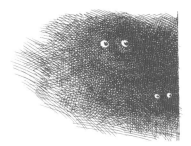

Suddenly the front door creaked open.

Grandpa put a finger to his lips and pulled Benny into the shadows.

In walked a man in a tattered coat.
He took the bag of bagels from the Ark.

"O Lord, I was so hungry," he sobbed. "For weeks
You fed me. From heaven You sent such beautiful bagels."

He tucked the bag under his coat.

"I have good news for both of us," he said. "I have found work."

He wiped away his tears.

"Now I can feed myself and You can stop baking bagels."

The man smiled as he quietly closed the cupboard.

"You helped me Lord. Now I promise to help others."

Then he left.

Benny buried his face in Grandpa's coat and wept.

"God didn't eat my bagels. That poor man took them."

Grandpa's eyes grew wide with wonder.

"Benny," he asked. "You wanted to thank God?"

"Yes." Benny sniffed.

"Well, you did," said Grandpa.

"How?" Benny asked.

"Didn't you give bagels to a hungry man?" asked Grandpa.

"Yes," Benny replied.

"Didn't he promise to help others?"

"Yes." Benny nodded.

"Then you made the world a little better," said Grandpa.

"I did?" Benny wondered.

"You did." Grandpa smiled.

"And what better thanks could God have?"

To Alec Gelcer for the recipe and Susan Josephs for the fire — A.D.
For Dragana, who understands — D.P.

BAGELS FROM BENNY has its roots in an ancient Jewish folk tale from Spain. That story later became a legend featuring the 16th century Jewish Mystic Isaac Luria. In the 17th century, Rabbi Moses Hagiz of Amsterdam recorded a version of the tale.

Published in Canada and the U.S. by Kids Can Press Ltd.
25 Dockside Drive, Toronto, ON M5A 0B5

Kids Can Press is a Corus Entertainment Inc. company

www.kidscanpress.com

The artwork in this book was rendered in watercolor and pencil on 140 lb Fabriano watercolor paper. The text is set in Garamouche.

Edited by Debbie Rogosin
Designed by Marie Bartholomew and Dušan Petričić

Printed and bound in Tseung Kwan O, NT, Hong Kong, China, in 2/2021 by Paramount Printing Co. Ltd.

CM 03 0 9 8 7 6 5 4
CM PA 05 0 9 8

LIBRARY AND ARCHIVES CANADA CATALOGUING IN PUBLICATION

Davis, Aubrey
Bagels from Benny / written by Aubrey Davis ;
illustrated by Dušan Petričić.
ISBN 978-1-55337-417-6 (bound)
ISBN 978-1-55337-749-8 (pbk.)

1. Bagels — Folklore. 2. Jews — Folklore. 3. Tales — Spain.
I. Petričić, Dušan II. Title.

PS8557.A832B33 2003   jC813'.54   C2002 905545-8
072131.2K8/B1063/A5

Kids Can Press gratefully acknowledges that the land on which our office is located is the traditional territory of many nations, including the Mississaugas of the Credit, the Anishnabeg, the Chippewa, the Haudenosaunee and the Wendat peoples, and is now home to many diverse First Nations, Inuit and Métis peoples.

We thank the Government of Ontario, through Ontario Creates; the Ontario Arts Council; the Canada Council for the Arts; and the Government of Canada for supporting our publishing activity.